Lady Grace
And
The Evil Forest

THE LADY GRACE CHRONICLES

By
L.G.

For all women around the world who have been
abused, neglected, and tortured by governments or cultures, by family or society, we are
so much stronger than they know and when are – all of us – empowered, this world will
be saved at last.

ISBN 978-0-9904131-0-3

Distributed through CreateSpace, on-demand publishing, LLC

Lady Grace
And
The Evil Forest

THE LADY GRACE CHRONICLES

By
L.G.

"I can't take this shit anymore. She winced. "Sorry. That'll be the last time I cuss, I swear." She winced again. "No pun intended. I'm trying to quit."

He laughed.

"But here's the thing. I'm not. I am not going to take it anymore."

He nodded.

He was Harout Mohammed, a professor at Modibbo Adama University in Nigeria who had devoted himself to studying the political and familial culture of Boko Haram, a seemingly new terrorist group kidnapping school girls and terrorizing the nation. In truth, Boko Haram had been around for decades but only recent events and the ever-reaching world of the Internet had now brought them global notoriety and the interest of Lady Grace.

The man and woman studied each other.

His English was perfect and so the translator had been left outside his office. Her payment had been immense and so security was stationed outside as well. But this arrangement was unorthodox. A Muslim man and an unrelated, unaccompanied woman alone in his office would be frowned upon by many. But she had said her name was Lady Grace and she had paid well for his time.

They regarded each other.

Dr. Mohammed was nearly six feet tall, thick, heavily muscled but also fattened by an easy lifestyle. He was academia, the upper echelon of society in war-torn Nigeria. His skin was so dark there was almost a bluish hue that made his eyes and teeth appear impossibly white. He was, she decided, very handsome.

She was unusually slender, almost angular. She was his most perfect example of the cultural differences between their two nations. In Nigeria, a more fatty diet was a sign of prominence and wealth. It was good to live as a fat king. But in her world, in the world of Lady Grace, living with a lean body with very little body fat was a symbol of status and fortune. How at odds they were, their worlds.

Her hair was a deep red with thick waves that could no more be tamed than the wilds of Sambisa Forest, the purpose of her visit. Yet it was because of this, because of her hair that Dr. Mohammed somehow believed in this woman.

"You cannot believe that you can simply walk into the forest," he told her.

"Why not?" She was indignant.

"Well … because." He almost laughed. It was absurd. "Sambisa is called the Evil Forest for a reason. It is like no other. It has some of the most poisonous snakes in the world, the most vicious animals," he said. And it was for this reason alone that Sambisa Forest had been home to robbers and smugglers for more than a century for no one else would dare follow them into the Evil Forest. Covering more than 23,000 square miles, the forest, nestled in the northeastern corner of Nigeria, connected with Chad, Cameroon and Niger, making it easy for criminals to disappear into the dense bush.

"From the moment your people step foot into the forest, you will be known," Dr. Mohammed warned. "It is a place of terror and the Boko Haram have made it their home. They know the terrain well, better than the Nigerian military, and can melt easily into it; yet they can just as easily appear in surrounding villages and local populations that they have terrorized before. This is their land; it is their territory." As he spoke, his voice rose to almost a high-pitch shout.

"It is also where they have taken the girls," Lady Grace said.

"Perhaps."

"Perhaps?" Her eyebrows rose as she studied him.

He sighed.

"Yes. They are there. The girls. They are there."

"Again, please tell me how you know this," Lady Grace said. She had taken a seat opposite of his desk. She had done so without permission, without hesitation, while he continued to stand. She was a lady of wealth and prominence, one who knew or cared nothing of another culture that would discourage such entitlement by a woman.

Dr. Mohammed noted that while she waited for her answer, she did not bother to give him eye contact but, instead, studied the books that lined his bookshelves. Beneath her covering, he could see that she was muscular and lean. Though the fabric modestly covered her body, it was so sheer that Dr. Mohammed could see the tan of her skin, the sleeveless blouse, and form-fitting trousers.

"Some of the girls escaped," he said.

"How many?" she asked, still studying his bookshelves.

"More than 50 managed to escape. You asked me this before," he said, and her attention snapped back to him.

"Did I?" she asked.

He nodded.

"You're sure it was me?" He nodded again, though with a little uncertainty. "Many have been asking about these girls. It has made global news. How can you be so sure it was me you spoke to?" Her gaze was hard and, quite suddenly, he was reminded of something she had said to him earlier, and he looked away. He fumbled for his chair and, at last, took a seat so they were seated eye to eye. She asked again, "How many?"

"Boko Haram kidnapped more than 200. Just how many, we cannot be sure. There are many families who have not yet reported their daughters missing, so we cannot be entirely sure, but we know over 200 girls have been taken from their secondary school in the northeast of Nigeria. Boko Haram's leader, Abubakar Zahier, has taken them to the Sambisa Forest for both cover and protection. There, he can use the girls as human shields if troops are sent in, he can rape them, he can torture them, and he has promised to give them as gifts to new recruits but he also threatens to sell them on the market as slaves and prostitutes.

"We do not know from the girls who escaped where all the girls are now. It does appear that Abubakar Zahier has already split the girls up into groups of ten or 12, so they can be spread out throughout Sambisa, making rescue attempts much more difficult." He sighed heavily. "It will not be easy to go in and simply rescue these girls. You will need to have troops on the ground that are willing to go into the unknown, go into the Evil Forest and be willing to die fighting something they cannot even see. This is not to mention the snakes, the spiders, the animals that will attack."

Lady Grace smiled and nodded thoughtfully, making a slight humming sound. Almost a minute ticked off the clock that sat on Dr. Mohammed's desk. He was mesmerized. Lady Grace, whoever she was, had nerves of steel.

"This is why I came to you," she said. "For such insight."

More time ticked on the clock.

"Today," Dr. Mohammed spoke, unable to bear the silence any longer, "the United States has announced they are sending soldiers and experts who specialize in intelligence, rescue operations, and hostage negotiations."

She laughed.

"You are English?" he guessed and her gaze drifted from him to his books and back to him again. She was not going to answer.

"Not American," he continued, trying to puzzle out her accent, her demeanor, her appearance. She smiled.

"You are not going into Sambisa?" It was more of a statement than a question but, still, Lady Grace said nothing.

"Boko Haram has been terrorizing this nation for decades, burning down churches, killing almost 2,000 people each year, burning schools with children locked inside. They do this because they hate anything or anyone Western, they say. Boko Haram means, quite literally translated, 'Western education is sinful.' This is how much hate they have for anything of the Western hemisphere."

"And they won't stop until Nigeria is an Islamic state," she said and he nodded, breathing out. He was relieved. He had begun to feel he was the only one participating in the conversation.

"That is correct! But they are not Muslim. Not to my mind. I am Muslim, and I do not believe in what they are doing."

Lady Grace nodded again.

"And what about your government? Why have they allowed this group to continue the way it has?" she asked.

He shrugged. "I do not think … you must understand. It is what I have told you. Boko Haram can disappear into the night and reappear just as mysteriously. They are boys and men, neighbors, and mere travelers. Who is one? Who is not? How do you catch what you cannot see? How do you know what you are seeing?"

"Especially when you're not really trying," Lady Grace added and Dr. Mohammed snapped his mouth closed. He did not disagree. He could not disagree. Another minute ticked off the clock.

"I must ask," Dr. Mohammed said at last. "What is it that you want from me?"

"The girls who escaped— "

"Yes."

"You interviewed them?" she asked, though she already knew the answer. She had read the complete file. She had read several of the interviews. She had been privy to information that most in the world had not. She had paid a pretty penny to ensure weapons, recon equipment, soldiers of fortune and select military personnel were all at her disposal but not before she had thoroughly researched Boko Haram, its leader, Dr. Harout Mohammed, and local militia.

She stood.

As if on cue, the door opened and three men entered. But Lady Grace never took her eyes off of Dr. Mohammed. One of the men stepped forward, withdrawing a folder from the inside of his jacket, and placed two pictures on Dr. Mohammed's desk.

"I want access to these two women," Lady Grace pointed.

"Abalunam Ndikumana," Dr. Mohammed said, frowning at the first picture. It was the picture of a young girl, anywhere from 13 to 16 years old. Like Dr. Mohammed, her skin was an inky black. She had large brown eyes that showed no emotion, not fear, not joy, not contentment, or resentment. She was a beautiful blank slate.

Lady Grace slid the second picture forward and Dr. Mohammed's frown deepened.

"Kamka Okoro."

This girl was a little older, more mature, and more expressive. A quiet rage exuded from the picture. She was a round-faced beauty with high cheekbones, almond shaped eyes, and a mouth drawn so tightly she looked as though she were stifling a scream. This had been the picture that Lady Grace had studied the entire flight over the Indian Ocean and the long commute into Nigeria, to the university. This had been the face that spoke to her in her sleep, in her waking hours. This was the face that fueled her own rage.

"How?" Dr. Mohammed looked up quizzically. "How do you possess these pictures?"

"You have been paid very handsomely not to ask but to answer questions, Dr. Mohammed," Lady Grace said.

He shook his head, frowning at the pictures again.

"But no one has—."

"Introduce me to Abalunam and Kamka." She shrugged. "Then, you will be free of us. It's that simple."

And he would be, but not before he asked one more question. It was morbid curiosity, nothing more. But, when the answer came, he had been sorry he asked.

"This is a land rich with deceit and corruption, Lady Grace. How do you know that I will not report your arrival and your intentions?" After all, how would she know? For all her money and power, prestige and hired guns, she did not know Nigeria. She could not imagine the level of corruption that was the way of life in this land. But he had been wrong.

She smiled once more and, without ever speaking a word, extended a hand to one of her men who produced yet another file. This one, however, was closed. She slid it across his desk with just one finger, smiling as she did. It was an alluring, almost teasing smile.

As he opened the file she said, "Because I'll kill everyone and everything you ever loved." Indeed, Lady Grace had photos and information on everyone and everything he had ever loved.

Chapter Two

Abalunam had been difficult to persuade but Lady Grace knew this would be the case going in and, for this reason, she had approached Kamka first. She had read Dr. Harout Mohammed's interview with the escapees. She had read the police reports, such as they were, and the news threads by various reporters. But these were just words. She did not need words. She needed sight and sound, smell and intuition. If she was going to pull this off, if she was going to go into the bowels of the Evil Forest and hunt down that shithole Abubakar Zahier and wipe him off the face of this earth, she needed a lot more than words. Of the bunch who had escaped, her team had identified these two as the best candidates.

Initially, Kamka had been extremely skeptical and then horrified at the notion of returning to Sambisa Forest, but then that rage that Lady Grace had studied, believed in and counted on had returned to Kamka's pretty face. It was a sweet, silent pitiless rage that would drive Kamka right back into the camp of her captors only so that she could witness the slaughter. She had needed assurances that the others would be saved, that she would not be recaptured and that no other girl would suffer, but beyond that she made no demands. She wanted no money. She had listened to Lady Grace's plan; she had seen the arsenal and had agreed to be a guide. It was Abalunam who had surprised Lady Grace. For the first twenty minutes, she had rocked back and forth, wailing and screeching, refusing even to think about what lay in the Sambisa Forest. Then, as suddenly as it had all begun, she had stopped crying and looked at Lady Grace with just one demand.

"If I lead you to them and you find Abubakar Zahier and his men, you must promise me this," she said and her gaze floated from Lady Grace to her 1st Lieutenant, a giant of a man, ex-Marine, professional boxer and ruthless mercenary who held allegiance only to money, his faith and his word. "You have to promise me that you will shove the AK-47 that they love so much inside them and pull the trigger."

Kamka mumbled under her breath, and Abalunam lifted her gaze again to the 1st Lieutenant and clarified her previous statement. "I do not mean in his stomach or mouth but into his bottom."

"And pull the trigger," Kamka said quietly.

"Yes, ma'am," the 1st Lieutenant said. "Not a problem."

Lady Grace was well aware of the horrific stories of rape by way of AK-47. In particular, Abubakar Zahier favored sodomizing women with the end of his weapon, all the while contemplating whether to pull the trigger or not as he shredded the vagina and inner organs of his helpless victims.

"And you make me this promise," Lady Grace said in return. "When we have done this, you will deliver a message for me."

"It is a promise I will keep," Kamka said when she heard what it was Lady Grace wanted her to do.

And so they set off just as the girls had only two weeks before, in the middle of the night, with nothing more than the shoes and the clothes they wore. Lady Grace and her team, however, had things that gave the girls renewed courage and hope. Beyond the weapons and water canteens, there were duffel bags of unknown items, shovels, camera equipment and, as they journeyed, more and more men fell in to step with them until they had walked across the savanna almost an hour, far from the village that was home.

On the night of their abduction, Abubakar Zahier had loaded the girls into a caravan of trucks. He had laughed as he did so, shouting to the night's sky that with his fleet of trucks, no one would ever see the girls again, that no one could match his power, and no one would ever stop him in his rise to fame. He proclaimed that Allah spoke to him, that Allah had told him to sell the girls as they were mere trinkets in the joys of warfare and reclaiming justice. Nigeria was a land of cowards and he could take any boy, any girl and do with them what he liked. Indeed, he had. But on this night, Kamka and Abalunam saw that Lady Grace also had a fleet of trucks, though much smaller, but they were far more organized.

Little was known of Abubakar Zahier, including his appearance which reportedly changed each time he made and posted a video to taunt the world. Abubakar Zahier was different from many Islamic Fundamentalists in that his message was not the typical non-expressive, monotone speech of infidels and paying the almighty price. Instead, he was animated. Almost boyish. He laughed as he spoke of human sufferings, slavery, and bondage.

In the last seven years, there had been three different reports of Abubakar Zahier's death by Nigerian militants but he continued to resurface, each time becoming more violent, more jubilant. His kidnappings were becoming increasingly brazen, his attacks increasingly brutal. His appearance ever changing. And so it was for this reason that Lady Grace needed the girls to help identify not only the passage into Sambisa Forest but Abubakar Zahier himself.

Lady Grace watched the young girls giggle as they were fitted with night vision goggles. Still children themselves, despite the horrors they escaped and the certain terror they were to reenter, they delighted in the new toys. Lady Grace could not help but smile as she watched both girls, headsets in place, wildly swinging their arms around in the dark, pretending to hit each other all because they had sight – magical sight in the darkness. But, by the time they reached the edge of Sambisa Forest, all play had subsided. No one spoke but, from time to time, Kamka would offer a nod or shake of the head to determine the direction in which they traveled.

They were being watched. Wearing two-way radio sets sewn into their Kevlar vests, Lady Grace, her 1st and 2nd lieutenants and a man known only as Honey Bear, communicated along the trek. Honey Bear identified the different animal species that watched them from afar, always on the lookout for human eyes. There had been none. At least, none that he had seen. While Abalunam was uncertain from time to time, whether from fear or geographical disorientation, Kamka never faltered. As the night wore on, Kamka did not relent. She charged forward, her right arm rotating forward and forward like a windmill, through the thick brush, urging the troops on. If she had any concerns about poisonous snakes, Lady Grace determined, Kamka had overcome them in her burning desire to find the camp of rebels and her missing sisters. Even before they set out, Kamka had taken Lady Grace's arm once more and whispered to her that she must keep her promise.

"You will kill them all?"

"No one but your sisters will leave the camp," Lady Grace had said. It had been all that Kamka needed to hear before she led the way. So when she did, at last, find the trail that led them to the rebel's campsite and they heard the faraway chants and laughter of rebel men and boys drunk from both substance and the power of brutality, Kamka turned on her heel toward Lady Grace. Though Lady Grace knew that Kamka could no longer see in the darkness, both understood the gesture when Kamka pulled off her night goggles. She wanted Lady Grace to see her face – her full expression – as she pointed into the darkness. Beyond her fingertip was hell and terror and evil, and now it was Lady Grace's turn to keep her promise.

"Honey Bear," Lady Grace said into her radio. "Send teams two and three out. Lieutenant, have Kamka and Abalunam hold. Lieutenant Scott, talk to me."

In the distance, there was a scream of a young girl followed by raucous male laughter.

Lieutenant Scott, her second in command, laid out the instructions that would perfectly place each man in position and, within mere minutes, Lady Grace had readied herself behind who she believed was Abubakar Zahier. She was at least 60 meters from the man, but she was sure it was him. In those torturously long moments, there were two occasions when Abubakar Zahier held up his hand to silence his gang of thugs to listen to the forest. Both times had been ineffectual as the naked girl, no more than twelve, continued to whimper and cry despite the hand that first muffled her mouth and then viciously slapped it. The slap worked to the advantage of Lady Grace and her men as the girl wailed even louder, and Abubakar Zahier found that more amusing than any concern he might have from within the forest.

Her senses, all her senses, were immediately assaulted at the sight of the rebel's camp. She wanted to vomit. She wanted to scream. She wanted to cry. She wanted to burst from her hiding position and open fire on every motherfucker there, imagining each head exploding as her bullets ripped open their skulls and faces.

Beyond the whimpering girl, Lady Grace could see a makeshift tent with girls huddled inside, each one crying. At the mouth of the tent, another girl lay on her back, eyes wide open yet making no sound while a boy, no more than twelve himself, furiously humped her. Two standing boys cheered him on as he slammed against her small body.

To the left, another 20 meters from the girl's tent, three other boys or young men were gang raping another girl. Unlike the other, this girl had been forced to her knees and, while she was assaulted from behind, another young man had placed himself before the girl forcing his penis in her mouth. As she gagged and cried, they laughed.

Lady Grace could smell bile. It was her own. She could smell her own stomach churning and producing acids that were putrid. She could smell the forest, the burning embers of a now fading fire. She could smell sweat and heat, grass and dirt. But it was the sounds. The sounds. She could hear her own breathing, a rising panic as violence poured over the girls. She could hear the cries and the whimpers and the screams. But it was the laughter that roared in her ears and ravaged her brain, scraping and gnawing at the inside of her head so loudly that perhaps this was why she never heard Kamka coming.

They were not yet fully in place.

They were not ready.

They had not given the signal. Then, there she was, breaching the inner circle of the rebel camp, screaming and wildly waving a knife. Where had she gotten a knife? A man closest to whom Lady Grace believed to be Abubakar Zahier stepped forward and, without losing a step, Kamka sunk the knife into his chest.

No smells.

No sounds.

No more whimpers, no screams.

Everything and everyone stopped to watch as the man stood perfectly still and slowly looked down at his own chest and stared at the knife as a red stain slowly spread out over his shirt. He looked up and laughed. He laughed. And then all hell broke loose.

Honey Bear was three steps behind Kamka. At the sight of a large white man in fatigues, the rebels were on their feet, yelling, and drawing weapons. Honey Bear knew, as did they all, they were on an ask-no-questions mission where no prisoners were to be taken. He opened fired and bodies fell.

Chapter Three

Dr. Harout Mohammed once again found himself seated before the two young girls called Kamka Okoro and Abalunam Ndikumana. As a leading historian and researcher of the Boko Haram, it was logical that he speak to the survivors of the rebel slaughter. It was expected, however, that the girls would first speak to the police, to the militia and government officials. The president of Nigeria had just days before made the global announcement that the kidnapping of the schoolgirls would be the beginning of the end for the terrorists. He proclaimed that the nation of Nigeria would be terrorized no longer.

In the eyes of the world, the president had made good on his words when first stories of Abubakar Zahier's death and then pictures of the rebel camp were revealed. The international community applauded the Nigerian government, and its president basked in the glory of all that was right and just for the girls of his country. But Kamka and Abalunam knew the truth and, following the instructions of Lady Grace, refused to speak to anyone but Dr. Harout Mohammed.

"So," he said to both girls, penned poised in his hand, "please tell me before we proceed. Why is it that you will only speak to me?"

"It was a promise and so we are here. She made good on her promise and we will do the same," Abalunam said.

"And what was her promise to you?" Dr. Mohammed asked.

Initially, he wrote detailed notes as the women spoke of their trek to Sambisa Forest and finding the trail. As they described what happened next, his pen stopped. It was not a conscious thought. It was that he had forgotten he had a pen in his hand. It was the passion of the girls' stories, their excitement, and joy and unapologetic description of how they watched Abubakar Zahier succumb to the rape by his own AK-47. It was how Kamka described withdrawing her knife from the rebel, how he fell, and yet another rebel ran toward her only to be shot to pieces before her very eyes by Lady Grace. And while Kamka described in most vivid detail how a man called Honey Bear abandoned his own rifle in favor of a machete so that he could hack to pieces the boys and men who had tortured her sisters, Abalunam explained how she ran to the girl's tent and set them free. The girls, all of them, dozens upon dozens upon dozens, ran screaming from the rebel camp back into the Evil Forest to escape the terror and never looked back to see that there was no longer anything to fear.

The man, the big man who had promised Abalunam that he would assault each rebel with his own weapon, had made good on his promise as he moved like a leopard, first shooting and then stabbing and then hacking each body so that it was reduced from being to corpse to chunks of meat and discarded bone, decapitated and mutilated flesh. It was a sea of blood, a river of disemboweled organs and slow suffering agony, and Dr. Mohammed sat frozen in stupefied wonderment as Kamka clapped her hands in extreme satisfaction.

12

It was only when Kamka blinked that Dr. Mohammed realized that the story was over. He found both girls looking at him with a measure of curiosity. They were waiting for him to speak, but he could think of nothing to say. How had this massacre been any different from what the terrorists were doing? As he viewed the pictures once more, he realized that this had not just been a slaughter but it was a showpiece. The carnage had not occurred just from revenge or hatred. It has been an orchestrated affair to teach a lesson and show the world that there was something bigger than Boko Haram.

At last, he found his voice.

"I suffered, too, when you girls were taken from us and I rejoiced upon your return, but I cannot celebrate this," he said, tapping the picture that lay on the table between then.

Abalunam and Kamka looked at each other for a moment. Abalunam shrugged.

"Please, Dr. Mohammed, sir. I mean no disrespect, but you could not have suffered as we did so you cannot celebrate as we do." Life, she assured him, would change. Women, she said, now understood that they must change. If they continued to live in fear, never fight back, never stand up or speak out, these atrocities against them would never end. Before Lady Grace, they had been too frightened to fight back. It had been taught to them by their fathers and uncles, brothers and husbands that they should never talk back to a man, not even a boy. It was their place, they had been taught, to bear children and serve husbands and village leaders. No more, the girls told him. They were more than that. They wanted more than that.

At some point, Dr. Mohammed once again found his pen and began to write. His hand floated across the paper, making notations he hardly remembered until much later when he prepared his transcripts.

The girls understood that while Abubakar Zahier was gone, another would come.

Abubakar Zahier had bragged that when one leader fell another would stand in his place. He and his group would continue its reign of terror until all infidels were destroyed. As Lady Grace had explained to them, it was no coincidence that Abubakar Zahier and others like him always settled in poorer regions where desperate people did desperate things for money and power. It was easy to convince a poor and uneducated man that he should be given more, but what Lady Grace could not understand was why so many governments of so many countries continued to allow women to be raped, burned, tortured, and killed in the name of "honor" or religion, for power or for sport. Only when the world asked about the kidnapped girls did Nigeria's president finally step forward to decry Boko Haram. But this was a new day. No more.

If reason and morality could not be used, Lady Grace would do just as the men had done for centuries, and use brutality and force.

Yes, the violent killings of Boko Haram in the Evil Forest had been by design. Not only were the girls found, something that the local militia said could not be done, but the rebels were on display for the world to see. While Abubakar Zahier had promised young men the gifts of women, guns, and power, Lady Grace now offered a new guarantee – a death so violent and bloodied, a body so violated and gruesome that Heaven's Gate would never open for it.

"The ghosts of the Sambisa Forest are headless," Kamka laughed. "They have no ears or eyes or tongues. They are eunuchs!"

13

The girls laughed together, startling Dr. Mohammed. He had never seen such behavior. Speechless, he peered down once again at the pictures before him and studied the mutilated bodies of the Boko Haram. He studied the picture of Abubakar Zahier. Then, he saw it. He had seen it all along, of course, but never noticed it. The body of Abubakar Zahier was not in the Evil Forest. It was not in the same location as the bodies of his fellow rebels but when he shared this observation out loud, he was surprised again.

The girls did not deny this. They did not act as though this was new information. Rather, they laughed again.

"Then, you know," Dr. Mohammed said. "You were there? You were there to see Abubakar Zahier killed?" he asked.

"We are not afraid any longer," Abalunam said, and she stood to leave. Without hesitation, Kamka also stood, surprising Dr. Mohammed, for they had not asked to be dismissed. Instead, they had appeared, he felt, almost disrespectful. He opened his mouth to say something when Kamka produced a note from a small pocket on her dress.

"What is this?" Dr. Mohammed asked.

"It is a note from Lady Grace. She asked that I give it to you," and Kamka turned to leave.

The note consisted of one question. It asked: Why were Kamka and Abalunam selected to find their enemy and rescue their sisters?

It was a question Dr. Mohammed had meant to ask Lady Grace in person but never had the chance. When he looked back up to the girls, he found that Abalunam had already left, leaving just Kamka at the door of his office.

"What do you know of Abubakar Zahier," he asked, pointing a finger to the picture on the table. She only shrugged.

"He got what he deserved."

Dr. Mohammed knew from the way she smiled that she would say nothing more of it but there was much more to the story. With that, she gave a small bow and started to leave.

"And where will you go now?" he inquired, wondering if she might return to her village or stay in the city. Kamka shrugged and smiled.

"Lady Grace will protect us."

"Lady Grace? She is coming back?" Dr. Mohammed asked, his pen held fast in his hand.

Kamka's smile broadened. "She is already here."

Chapter Four

Daniel Forester studied the pictures of the rebel camp and all its carnage. The very pictures had gone viral. One of the more popular pictures had become an Instagram hit of Abubakar Zahier's mutilated body with the headline: Abubakar Zahier is not impressed!

While the world appeared to delight in dead Abubakar Zahier jokes, Agent Forester had taken a particular interest in the pictures of Abubakar Zahier. His body was in a different location than his rebel colleagues. Presumably, Abubakar Zahier had been taken alive, then tortured and killed in a separate location.

Why?

By whom?

Agent Forester sat at his desk, swiveling back and forth in his chair, eyes glued to all the pictures scattered before him. They were not just pictures of Abubakar Zahier and his men but of a variety of killings, of different groups and people from around the world.

As he swiveled and contemplated, a young man in his late twenties poked his head and shoulders into Forester's small office. Forester brightened. He liked the kid. Tall, lean, blonde, bespectacled, sloppy in his shirt and tie but efficient in the office. Agent Rose could have been Forester's little brother.

"What'cha got?" he asked and Rose eased in to the office.

"Those names? Kind of interesting and it's probably nothing, but I was playing around with the names. You know, the Nigerians are heavy into meanings of names," Rose said and Forester nodded, waiting.

"Yeah. So," and Rose looked down at his notes again for proper pronunciation. "Abul-unam? That means, get this, the literal translation is 'Don't argument with me,' in Nigeria. And the other name? Kamka. It means, 'A youth who is seeking for better opportunity and for a good and secure future.' How crazy is that?"

Forester nodded, not at all surprised.

He had seen this before. There always seemed some tantalizing bit of information that accompanied the event or the people involved in these recent killings.

Rose moved closer to the desk and shuffled the pictures around, pulling up the killings in the Sambisa Forest.

"Anything new?" he asked and Forester shook his head.

There were scattered reports of a rogue militia group led by a woman, but those were all heavily denied by the Nigerian government which took full responsibility for the deaths of Abubakar Zahier and his men. There were a few mentions of a "Lady Grace," but the references were so convoluted that any reader could easily interpret them to mean a local church, a volunteer organization, a friend of the school from which the girls were initially kidnapped. But the name was there, nonetheless. Lady Grace. Despite the denials, the name was there.

Who was Lady Grace?

What was her interest in these regions of the world?

Moreover, how did a white, red-headed foreigner move so easily throughout the African continent without a paper trail? He found no evidence of a passport, no documentation with customs. While Nigeria was well known for its backroom deals, it was unusual not to turn over one photograph, one image, one piece of credible documentation of a Lady Grace.

Dr. Mohammed, however, was a very real and credible source. His reputation as a historian and researcher was stellar in the academic community. He was well versed in the ways of the Boko Haram movement and had confirmed just hours after Abubakar Zahier's death that a Lady Grace, tall and statuesque, red-headed with a penchant for cursing, had waltzed into his office asking questions about Abubakar Zahier. Then, just one day later, Dr. Mohammad denied all reports of such a person or any encounter with a Lady Grace.

"It's the damndest thing," he said. "There is a Lady Grace. I know it. There is a Lady Grace." But what was she? A redhead? Brunette? Black? White? More importantly, who was she? It was a mystery.

Chapter Five

Honey Bear had lifted Abubakar Zahier without effort. While gunfire and shouts echoed around them, Honey Bear simply moved in, grabbed the rebel leader and carried him to one of the trucks for transport.

At the truck, Lady Grace paused. She looked back over her shoulder to the destruction that lay behind her. Her men were doing exactly what they had been hired to do. Not one terrorist would be left to tell the tale of survival and twist the facts to suit his own version of history. There would be no talk of heroics, no last stance, no swearing revenge upon the infidels. The rebels were treated, at long last, as they had treated others. They would die without mercy and without pity. So when she saw a particular man crying out, weeping to be spared, she hesitated. She momentarily forgot Honey Bear and Abubakar Zahier and stopped to watch the pig of a man who had stolen children in the night to torture and rape them, to laugh at them as they cried for their mothers, to spit on them when they asked for water and tease them that they would be sold to faraway place to be whores when they asked for mercy. She stood transfixed. And when her own man slashed a blade across the tops of the man's thighs and then back again across his abdomen, Lady Grace nodded with certain satisfaction as the coward child killer was felled. She saw her own man then bend down to speak to the coward something which made him nod.

Lady Grace's man stiffened for a moment, instantly looking for his 1st Lieutenant. When he did, he spied Lady Grace watching and a smile swept across his face. At once, she understood. The coward had been asked if he understood that he was a coward, a child rapist, a disease set upon his own people and nation for a misguided, distorted and disgusting mission that was not a mission, not a truth but a cancer that was destroying the world. The rebel had nodded an affirmative.

Each rebel, it had been instructed, would die renouncing his cause, begging for forgiveness yet would receive none.

Her man plunged his knife into the neck of the coward and he bled out crying, in agony, terrified. Lady Grace's man took a picture.

In honor of the girls, the tents and the entire encampment was set ablaze. Each body, however, was carefully dragged to the edge of Sambisa Forest where the villagers, the parents of the girls and the girls themselves could come back and spit upon each body if they chose to do so. Word had also been put out to any man, woman or child who grieved for these sons of the devil's work that they would also be killed. The time had come that it was no longer permissible to know of, to house or feed a terrorist. A terrorist should never die with glory, with promise of an afterlife or grieving loved ones but he should die miserable and alone as a scourge.

As Lady Grace climbed into the truck, a fire raged and the cries of tortured men rang in her ears. The mission had been a success but even with the girls freed, there was one more task to be handled.

"We ready?" Honey Bear asked Lady Grace as she settled into her seat. She nodded.

Behind her were two more of her men and Abubakar Zahier, bound, gagged and bleeding in the belly of the truck.

Her other men would join up with them in less than 45 minutes. It was enough time to secure the scene, get plenty of photographic evidence, allow Lady Grace the time she needed with her own prisoner and still flee the country without detection. She looked back at Abubakar Zahier and hoped this would be enough time. While his eyes were filed with fury, she knew he had to be a scared. Twice, it had been reported, Abubakar Zahier had escaped death and so he had bragged that it was God's will he had been spared. For this reason, she wondered if he now prayed for help once more.

"God is not here right now," she leaned over the back of the seat and spoke to her prisoner. "He is rejoicing with the girls back at their village." Her Arabic was perfect.

He did not even blink.

She smiled to herself. Dr. Mohammed would be surprised to learn that she knew Arabic. He would be surprised by many of the things she knew. But her smile faded as she thought about the aftermath of all of this. Boko Haram was similar to al-Qaida in the way it was run. There were individual cells that each operated under the guise of al-Qaida or Boko Haram, each under its own leader.

It was true what Abubakar Zahier had said. When he was killed, another would come.

As if Honey Bear understood what his boss was thinking, he handed her the iPad that was sitting between them. When she took it, he tapped the screen with a large finger, instructing her to watch the very video they had viewed more than a dozen times. It was her reminder. It was her elixir.

It was of Abubakar Zahier, grinning into a camera proclaiming, "I have abducted the girls at a Western education school … I will sell them in the market, by Allah. There is a market for selling humans. Allah says I should sell; he commands me to sell. I will sell women. I sell women." And he laughed. Joyously.

While there were many cells and many leaders, Abubakar Zahier had worked magic in the terror department. He stole children. He killed children. He escaped capture and death and he laughed on camera. In the eyes of the world he was larger than life. In the realm of terrorism, Abubakar Zahier was a rising God.

"It is Allah that instructed us to do this!" Abubakar Zahier's voice spoke to Lady Grace from the screen. "Until we soak the ground of Nigeria with Christian blood and so-called Muslims contradicting Islam, we will not stop. After we have killed, killed, killed, and become so fatigued from our killing that we must wonder what to do with all the corpses, smelling of your Western leaders and your repugnant ways, we will open this prison here that we are in and we will imprison all others!" Again, he laughed.

What was worse was Abubakar Zahier was a handsome man. He was no bedraggled or withered but he was young, strong, handsome, well spoken. He was also completely insane.

So little was known of him. No one knew his exact age, level of schooling or who his family was. It was known only that he was born somewhere near the border between Nigeria and Niger, in the heart of the former Sokoto caliphate. It was said that he was always reading and was reportedly "scholarly." At an early age, he joined a group, as so many young Nigerian men do, with a rebel leader and quickly became of the one top lieutenants. And because there was no strong government in Nigeria, because corruption flourished in even the highest offices, it was easy for Boko Haram to flourish among the impoverished and educated. But now it was time for Lady Grace to make those same people understand that following terrorists, that living in fear, was no better than existing in a corrupt government. The people of Nigeria had to fight for a better life, not live with terrorism. The death of Abubakar Zahier would not be the answer but it would show them the light. The death of Abubakar Zahier would not end terrorism but it would show his victims that he could be stopped.

"I enjoy killing anyone that God commands me to kill," Abubakar Zahier beamed into the camera and he rocked his head back to give a good belly laugh.

Lady Grace squeezed her eyes shut for a moment, blocking the image of the girls being raped from her mind and she channeled her rage once more. Then, with a smile and a pleasant voice, she turned once more to speak to her prisoner.

"So, exactly how does this work … this way you think? How do you believe that Allah would have you raping little girls and then selling them off to be tortured and eventually killed?"

Nothing.

"You know yours is a false religion, right? You are not a true Muslim."

Nothing.

"I've studied the Muslim faith," she said and paused. This one, she knew, the idea of a woman studying the Muslim faith, would be particularly repulsive to Abubakar Zahier. "Yes. Well. I have studied it thoroughly, even consulted with sheiks and clerics and guess what? Your hate mongering, terror-pushing agenda is not the Muslim faith."

Nothing.

But his eyes were bulging and Lady Grace smiled.

"Yes. Yes. I have spoken to many, many clerics and they all assure me that you are an ignorant village boy who listened to crazy men who never had any formal education and because they cannot read the real Quran, they made things up and decided to teach that killing little girls was the way to Allah's heart. But, of course," and she laughed, "this is absurd and it is the reason that the entire world laughs at you and your ignorant brothers."

A small hiss released from Abubakar Zahier's mouth.

"Before this all comes to an end, I decided to give you a gift. You know, help you out since you've been so misguided. It's not your fault, really, I suppose, as you are just an ignorant little village boy. At least, this is what all the newspapers around the world say. They say when you laugh in your video that you are such a fool you do not even understand why you laugh."

The two men seated on either side of Abubakar Zahier were smiling and shaking their heads.

"Here goes. My gift to you. Killing babies? Bad. Helping out others? Good. Raping schoolgirls for sadistic, self-indulgent pleasures? Bad. Encouraging others to get an education to better themselves and help this nation thrive? Good. Locking little boys in a school and burning it down only to listen to them scream for help? Bad. Raising boys to be men of integrity, courage and strength? Good."

Nothing.

19

"Oh! Oh! Wait. You don't know what makes a man a man. Let's take a step back. A real man does not have sex with babies. A real man does not blow up school children or women shopping in the market to buy food for their families."

There was a movement by Abubakar Zahier and one of Lady Grace's men said, "I think something just popped in his head," and they all four laughed at the man on the floor.

Abubakar Zahier moved again, jerking his knees forward and then jutting them out as though he were trying to break the restraints.

"No, seriously," said Lady Grace's man. "I think he's convulsing."

The man spoke in English and there was no way for Abubakar Zahier to understand anything except that they were laughing at him but Lady Grace spoke once again in Arabic.

"It was probably too much 'how to be man' information coming at him all at once."

"It doesn't matter," Honey Bear said. His tone was low and flat, void of any emotion. "We're here."

Lady Grace turned to see they had come to the end of this mission. Honey Bear turned the truck engine off at the edge of the village they had previously identified. Not more than one hundred meters away were a group of women.

Without another word, Lady Grace's men pulled Abubakar Zahier from the truck and dragged him toward the women. Slowly, Lady Grace and Honey Bear emerged. Intentionally, Lady Grace trailed behind. She watched as each of her men hooked a hand under each of Abubakar Zahier's arms and dragged him across the dirt, clouds of dust pluming behind them, toward the small crowd. She could see Abubakar Zahier pick up his head, see the women, then curse to himself. He attempted to laugh. He hoped to instill that same fear he had on the Internet but to no avail. It was the turn of the women to laugh at him and Abubakar Zahier knew.

As he was dropped heavily to the ground before the women's feet, Abubakar Zahier knew that his time had come.

"Tell me," a woman said as she stepped forward. She bent down over Abubakar Zahier, purposefully shoveling dirt into his face. "When you laugh before the camera, what is it that you find so funny? Is it the attention that you receive, like that of a little boy who has all of his family to watch him as he performs a new trick? Or is it the idea of hurting so many that delights you?"

"He is so proud of his smile," another woman said, also kicking dirt as she stepped forward. "I should like to have those pretty white teeth. I, too, will laugh each time I see them. Perhaps I will make a necklace of them."

Abubakar Zahier gave a small cough as dust crept into his lungs and crawled down his throat. But there was no reprieve as yet another woman stepped forward, kicking dirt and sweetly suggesting that it was not his teeth she wanted but his shining, smiling eyes. She had heard that human eyes were worth thousands on the black market and she wondered how much the eyes of Abubakar Zahier would be worth?

As the women gathered around Abubakar Zahier, Lady Grace's men dropped back. They were there to make sure Abubakar Zahier did not run but the threat had been unnecessary as an old woman, wrapped in a burka, sliced both of his Achilles. While he writhed in agony, the women continued their calm discussion of body parts.

Lady Grace approached Kamka and Abalunam. Both of the girls stood to the side, arms folded across their chests and smiling.

"As-salamu alaykum," Lady Grace said.

"Salam," Kamka said with a small bow and all three women smiled upon one another. Lady Grace pondered Samka's most informal greeting which, loosely translated meant, "peace."

"Perhaps now," Lady Grace said and allowed the girls to understand her meaning. Words, particularly in this part of the world, were so important. Their meanings, their translations, their history, were all so very important.

A shrill scream made everyone stiffen yet Lady Grace, Abalunam and Kamka never looked to see what was happening.

"We cannot thank you enough, Lady Grace," Kamka began but Lady Grace waved her off.

"The hardest part is yet to come," she told the girls. "You know another will come."

They nodded.

"You must stay strong."

They nodded again and behind them another anguished cry escaped the man on the ground. Like an injured animal being picked apart by buzzards, the terrorist once known as Abubakar Zahier, was at last helpless. There was nothing he could do against his attackers and he could only hope for mercy. It was only a hope for he knew better than to ask.

"Your names are so special," Lady Grace told them. "Together, you are the new movement in Nigeria. Abalunam. Kamka." Lady Grace paused for effect, allowing the girls to fully hear their names, take in their true meanings and appreciate the moment that was theirs.

Honey Bear moved in, giving a small cough as their signal to go. Eyes still on the girls, Lady Grace nodded and stepped back. It was as she said. It was now their turn, their movement. One that represented fight and courage; one that stood for hope and for the future. Together, they embodied the spirit and soul of the Nigerian woman.

"Peace be with you," Abalunam and Kamka both said. Lady Grace gave a small bow and turned to leave. As she did, her gaze fell upon the last of the rebel called Abubakar Zahier and, quite unintentionally, she gave a sharp intake. Indeed, it was the last of the rebel once known as Abubakar Zahier and she smiled to herself. At the truck, she turned back to the girls.

"Peace be with you," she said and she was sure that it was so.

Postscript
(The Lady Grace Chronicles)

Though presented as fiction, *The Lady Grace Chronicles* is a response to real life events that are happening every day around the world. Today, right now, a female is being subjected to the greatest horrors simply because she is female and because there is no protection for her. No doubt, there is great violence against women in the Western "more civilized" countries but there does exists laws that prohibit rape, abuse, abduction and mutilation of women. Still, perverts and monsters dwell among us as does a twisted culture that stills objectifies women but these cases are for another story for another time.

The Lady Grace Chronicles looks at the countries (and cultures) that hold beliefs in family honor and sexual purity that justifies the torture, mutilation and murder of women. These same cultures have greater ideologies of male sexual entitlement, ownership and greater standing in their communities. The women who live in such cultures have no one and nothing to turn to. Local customs and its governing laws do not protect them against the most heinous of acts.

While ***Lady Grace and the Evil Forest*** deals with Islamic extremists, this is not a problem that centers around religion. Just as there is horrific violence against women in Pakistan, the same can be said of women half way around the world in the Ukraine, where human trafficking of women (for slave trade) is second only to the drug trade. In Gautamala and Belize, large billboards can be seen around the country warning its citizens of sex trafficking. These countries have very different religions, cultures, customs, languages, and climates but all share one commonality – the abuse of women.

It is not a coincidence that the countries that have gender equality and celebrate empowerment to women have better human right's records. These same countries that afford education to females have higher economic and social development. The lower the education for women, the fewer laws of protection for women, the more abuse women endure, the higher the poverty level for the country. Stifling economic and educational opportunities for women and hiding them behind archaic traditions hurts an entire nation. What does this tell us? It is time to change. It is time to stand up and speak out for our sisters around the world, not just for them but for the betterment of everyone.

THE END

Look for more The Lady Grace Chronicles in
the future! Become part of the movement.

www.ingramcontent.com/pod-product-compliance
Lightning Source LLC
Chambersburg PA
CBHW071232130626
46555CB00004B/1946